Pig Gets Stuck

Heather Amery

Illustrated by Stephen Cartwright

Language consultant: Betty Root
Series editor: Jenny Tyler

There is a little yellow duck to find on every page.

This is Apple Tree Farm.

This is Mrs. Boot, the farmer. She has two children, called Poppy and Sam, and a dog called Rusty.

On the farm there are six pigs.

The pigs live in a pen with a little house.
The smallest pig is called Curly.

It is time for breakfast.

Mrs. Boot gives the pigs their breakfast.
But Curly is so small, he does not get any.

Curly is hungry.

He looks for something else to eat in the pen.
Then he finds a little gap under the wire.

Curly is out.

He squeezes through the gap under the wire.
He is out in the farmyard.

He meets lots of other animals in the farmyard.
Which breakfast would he like to eat?

Curly wants the hens' breakfast.

He thinks the hens' breakfast looks good.
He squeezes through the gap in the fence.

Curly tries it.

The hens' food is so good, he gobbles it all up.
The hens are not pleased.

Mrs. Boot sees Curly.

Curly hears Mrs. Boot shouting at him.
"What are you doing in the hen run, Curly?"

He runs to the fence.

He tries to squeeze through the gap. But he has eaten so much breakfast, he is too fat.

Curly is stuck.

Curly pushes and pushes but he can't move.
He is stuck in the fence.

They all push.

Mrs. Boot, Poppy and Sam all push Curly.
He squeals and squeals. His sides hurt.

Curly is out.

Then with a grunt, Curly pops through the fence.
"He's out, he's out," shouts Sam.

He is safe now.

Mrs. Boot picks up Curly. "Poor little pig," she says. And she carries him back to the pig pen.

Curly is happy.

"Tomorrow you shall have lots of breakfast," she says. And Curly was never, ever hungry again.

Cover design by Hannah Ahmed   Digital manipulation by Natacha Goransky

This edition first published in 2004 by Usborne Publishing Ltd, 83-85 Saffron Hill, London EC1N 8RT, England. www.usborne.com